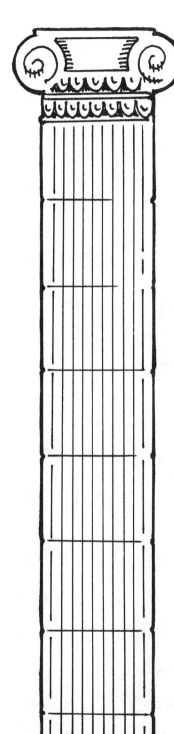

Ancient
Greece

Written by

Diane Sylvester

Illustrated by

Corbin Hillam

2 0 0 6 • T H E   L E A R N I N G   W O R K S

The Learning Works

Editor: Pam VanBlaricum
Illustrator: Corbin Hillam
Text Design: Acorn Studio Books
Cover Designer: Barbara Peterson
Cover Illustration: Gary Ciccarelli
Project Director: Linda Schwartz

The purchase of this book entitles the individual teacher to reproduce copies for use in the classroom. The reproduction of any part for an entire school or school system or for commercial use is strictly prohibited. No form of this work may be reproduced, transmitted, or recorded without written permission from the publisher.

Copyright © 2006 The Learning Works, Inc.

Contents

To the Teacher

Purpose

Museums are storehouses of interesting things that help us learn more about our natural and physical world. The purpose of this book is to provide ideas and activities to help students create their own museum full of specially crafted artifacts from ancient Greece.

The projects and activities in this book highlight the economic, political, social, scientific, and cultural components upon which all civilizations are based.

The projects and activities also provide these opportunities for students:

- Plan and give oral presentations

- Plan and conduct guided tours

- Plan and create graphs, labels, and posters

- Refine map reading skills

Social Studies Standards

The content of this book will allow the learner to meet the following social studies standards:

Identify characteristics (economy, social relations, religion, and political authority) of ancient Greek society.

Understand the connections between geography and city-states, including physical settings.

Explain the significance of Greek mythology to the people in the region.

Compare and contrast life in Athens and Sparta.

Describe the contributions of important Greek figures in the arts and sciences.

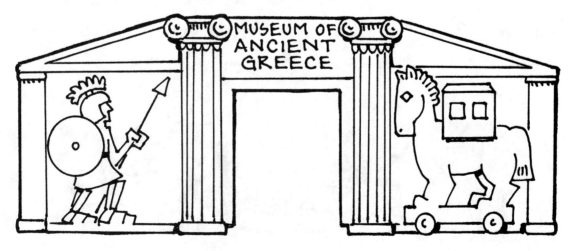

Tips and Ideas for Setting Up the Ancient Greece Museum

Creating a museum is often used as the culmination to a unit of study. However, creating a museum can be a unit by itself—full of educational and motivational activities and projects. The following ideas will help you and your students set up your ancient civilization museum.

Decisions to make before you begin

Where will the museum be located?

What roles will students assume in creating the artifacts and in displaying them?

How many artifacts will be included in the museum?

How will the students be grouped for each activity (individual, small group, or entire class)?

Suggestions for student roles

The teacher should decide whether or not to assume the roles of Museum Director and/or Curator.

Museum Director: assigns roles and coordinates lessons and activities

Curator: chooses the artifacts to be constructed and displayed; oversees placement of artifacts in museum; oversees labeling and educational material accompanying artifact

Design and Planning Specialists: students, or small groups of students, plan, make, and display artifacts

Public Education Advisors: students write scripts for tours; oversee training tour guides; and create advertising or educational videos

Advertisers: students create brochures, posters, advertisements, and invitations

Reporters: students write articles for class newspaper or other school publications

Tour Guides: students lead parents and other students on tour of museum

Ancient Greece © 2006 The Learning Works

Tips and Ideas for Setting Up
the Ancient Greece Museum *(continued)*

Suggestions for planning and creating your museum

Give your museum a creative name.

Make a large map of Greece.

Make a mural highlighting important achievements in ancient Greek history.

Consider making artifacts in a variety of ways—drawn, sculpted, carved, modeled, sewn, photographed, etc.

Consider using a variety of materials for the artifacts such as clay, papier mache, cardboard, wood, yarn, foil, etc.

The exhibit displays can be set on stands, put in boxes, hung from ceilings, attached to walls, placed on floors, etc.

Make signs for the museum—posters, bulletin boards, display stands, etc.

Publicize exhibit by creating pamphlets, posters, brochures, advertisements, videos, etc.

Create tour brochures, tour guide speeches, and audio tours.

Invite other classes and parents to the grand opening of the museum.

A day of festivities can mark the opening of the Ancient Greece Museum. Students can plan a parade complete with gods and goddesses, warriors, politicians, and boys and girls. Students should dress appropriately to represent people from different walks of life. Musicians and dancers can entertain. After the festival, participants can gather at Gorgon Grotto for a feast of olives, fruit, cheese, nuts, honey, and pita bread. Afterward, they can hold a "symposium" to discuss philosophical topics.

As part of the museum festivities, a special celebration can be held. Students can role-play their favorite god or goddess, tell a Greek myth, or act in a Greek play. Students can create their own dialogue. Think of a name for the event such the Mount Olympus Bash. Other components of the celebration can be costumes, food, music, and individual presentations.

Ancient Greece © 2006 The Learning Works

Invitation to the Grand Opening
of the Ancient Greece Museum

cut here

Celebrate the Grand Opening of the
 # Ancient Greece Museum

Date: _____   Time: _____

Location: _____

_____

Organized and Created by

_____

_____

_____

Exhibits • Displays • Ancient Artifacts • Personal Tours

cut here

Exhibit Description Card

Directions

Photocopy exhibit cards on heavyweight paper. Make one card per exhibit. Complete the information, fold the card, and place it alongside the museum artifact.

fold here

❦ Ancient Greece Museum ❦

Name of artifact: _____

Description: _____

_____

_____

_____

Designed and created by _____

Ancient Greece Project Proposal

Directions

Submit a completed *Ancient Greece Project Proposal* to your museum director or curator for approval.

Name(s): _____

Title of artifact/project: _____

Description of artifact/project: _____

_____

_____

What materials will you need? _____

_____

_____

How much room in the museum will your project need? _____

Write a short script describing the artifact/project for a museum tour guide to use.

_____

_____

_____

_____

Ancient Greece © 2006 The Learning Works

Brochure for the Grand Opening of the Ancient Greece Museum

Directions

Design a brochure or flyer that describes the exhibits in your museum. You may use the clip art on this page or draw your own illustrations.

Techniques for Creating Artifacts

Papier Mache Projects

Papier mache projects are easy to make—basically layering of paper over a shape—but can be messy and take several days to dry. Instant papier mache products are available from craft stores.

Materials

Pulp: Newspaper is a key ingredient for the papier mache pulp. Newspaper can also be used for creating details such as appendages, decorations, or facial features. Other types of papers can be used too, such as paper towels, tissue paper, and toilet paper. Some people recommend using brown paper bags because they are cleaner to use. Interesting effects can be achieved with fancy wrapping papers.

Paste: There are many different recipes for papier mache paste. Two of the easiest are ordinary liquid starch or a mixture of one part water with two parts white glue.

Shaped forms
You can create forms (armature or skeleton) for your papier mache projects from these suggested items:

   toilet paper and paper towel rolls
   egg cartons
   balloons (pop when papier mache is dry)
   aluminum pie pans
   paper cups
   cardboard boxes such as cereal boxes, oatmeal containers,
     and shoe boxes
   crumpled or rolled newspapers
   crunched aluminum foil

Other materials
   masking tape for holding the form components together
   bowl for paste
   scissors
   brushes to brush on paste, if preferred
   tempera or poster paints and paint brushes
   decorating items such as crepe paper, ribbons, glitter,
     beads, yarn, gold foil, old jewelry, etc.

Techniques for Creating Artifacts *(continued)*

Directions

1. Design the artifact on paper and then create the form out of suggested materials.

2. Tear or cut paper into strips.

3. Pour paste into a bowl. Dip each strip into the paste a few seconds, but don't soak it.

4. Place the strip where you want it on the form and smooth it down. Let the first layer dry thoroughly before adding another layer. It will also work to apply three or four layers before letting it dry, especially if time is short.

5. Use crushed or rolled newspaper to make appendages or other attachments. Use masking tape to attach these to the form. Papier mache the attachments.

6. Use pieces of newspaper to thicken features, or use wadded up paper pulp to form features.

7. Apply a final layer of white paper (paper towels, white tissue paper) so that the paint goes on easier. Use brown paper toweling for a different effect.

8. Let the artifact dry completely, and then paint it.

9. When the paint has dried, embellish the artifact with decorative items, if desired.

 Ancient Greece © 2006 The Learning Works

Techniques for Creating Artifacts *(continued)*

Clay Projects

Clay can be manipulated into many shapes and designs and is a perfect medium for making ancient civilization artifacts. Try to find clay that doesn't require baking or firing to save time and to make the process easier.

Materials:

Modeling clay or clay and sculpting materials that
  don't require firing or baking. Several types
  will dry bone hard and can be decorated,
  painted, and modified by sanding or filing.
tools for sculpting
toothpicks
paring knife or utility blade
coffee stirrers
cuticle sticks
textures from fabrics, window screen,
  sandpaper, emery boards, etc.
plastic forks and knives
craft sticks
grater for making hair
rolling pin for brayer

Directions

1. Decide on the size and type of artifact you will sculpt. You'll probably need 1–2 pounds of clay for each large artifact. Store extra clay in a sealable plastic bag or in a container with a lid. With air-dry clay, it is important to cover it with a wet cloth when not working on it.

2. Keep your sculpture on a piece of board or thick paper while working on it. Use the pinch method to anchor it to the base. Make it solid for stability.

3. Begin by rolling or forming clay to create the main part of the artifact.

4. Make appendages by rolling clay into a ball or rolling out "worms." Push a piece of clay through a cheese grater to make hair or other features.

5. Add details by using some of the tools suggested above.

6. Keep your artifact in its original clay color, or paint it in realistic colors.

Techniques for Creating Artifacts *(continued)*

Foil Projects

Foil works well for making artifacts because it is easy to create a good basic shape. It has volume and can be worked and reworked until you get the shape you want.

Materials

aluminum foil
permanent ink marking pens
masking tape
paint and brushes
cardboard
scissors
glue

Directions

1. On a sheet of paper, make a plan that details the components of the project.

2. Use foil to create the objects in your project. Gently crumple foil together. If you squeeze too hard, the foil compresses and the person or animal gets too thin.

3. Use extra pieces of foil to strengthen arms and legs.

4. Take the masking tape and completely cover each person or animal model.

5. A thick layer of papier mache can be applied over the masking tape. Otherwise, paint over the masking tape and draw in authentic details.

Ancient Greece © 2006 The Learning Works

Ancient Greece:
The Cradle of Civilization

Greece is a country made up of mainland Greece and many islands scattered throughout the Aegean and Ionian seas. All of the ancient Greeks shared a single language and religion, yet Greece was not a united country. Ancient Greece was divided into independent city-states; each city-state was ruled from one central city. Some of the city-states were Athens, Corinth, Sparta, Thebes, Delphi, and Olympia.

The ancient Greeks excelled in literature, drama, art, philosophy, mathematics, and science. They are also remembered for other contributions like the Olympic Games, trials by jury, and democratic government.

Today we see evidence of Greek culture all around us. Our democratic system of government, the architecture of public buildings, and the stories of Greek mythology are just a few examples.

Project Description

Make a relief map of ancient Greece out of papier mache (pages 12–13). The map should include the city-states of Athens, Sparta, Corinth, Thebes, Delphi, and Olympia; the Aegean Sea, the Ionian Sea, and the Mediterranean Sea; and other places pertinent to the artifacts in the museum. Display the map in a prominent location such as near the entrance to the museum.

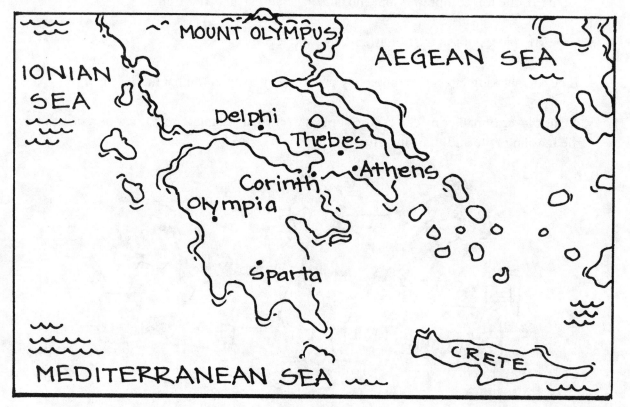

Timeline of Ancient Greek History

Ancient Greece was always a land of travelers—the early Greeks depended on the seas and were skillful sailors. Greeks sailed long distances to trade, to conquer new lands, or to seek new homes. This is the reason why some of the best preserved ancient Greek temples are found in southern Italy and Sicily. Ancient Greek civilization was at its most powerful between 800 and 146 B.C. when it was taken over by the Romans.

Events in Ancient Greek History

(Dates vary according to the criteria used by different archaeologists and historians.)

Archaic Period 800–500 B.C.

First Olympic Games
First known laws written by Draco
Coin currency introduced
Panathenaic festivals established
Democracy established by Cleisthenes

Classical Period 500– 400 B.C.

Persian wars made Athens strongest
    city-state
Delian League founded—an ancient
    equivalent to the North Atlantic
    Treaty Organization (NATO)
Age of Pericles, a soldier and statesman
Peloponnesian War ends Athens' dom-
    inance in Greece
Athens surrenders to Sparta
Parthenon is built

Late Classical Period 400–330 B.C.

Warfare between rival Greek leagues
Thebes defeats Sparta, dominates
    Greece briefly
Alexander the Great's reign begins
Plato founds Academy
Aristotle opens Lyceum

Hellenistic Age 330–30 B.C.

First Roman victories over Greece
Macedonian Wars: Greece becomes
    province of the Roman Empire
Corinth destroyed by the Romans
Athens is sacked by Sulla, a famous
    Roman general

Project Description

When you write the description card for each item in your museum, try to include the time period in which it was invented, built, or gained popularity.

Greek Alphabet

The Greek alphabet has been in continuous use for nearly 3,000 years. The Greeks borrowed and adapted the Phoenician alphabet, and created a writing system for their own language by modifying some letters representing sounds not found in Greek. The Greek alphabet evolved over several centuries, and by the 5th century B.C. it used 24 letters—17 consonants and 7 vowels. The name "alphabet" comes from the first two letters of the Greek alphabet, *alpha* and *beta*.

Greek letter		Name	English equivalent	Greek letter		Name	English equivalent
Α	α	alpha	a	Ν	ν	nu	n
Β	β	beta	b	Ξ	ξ	xi	ks, x
Γ	γ	gamma	g	Ο	ο	omicron	o
Δ	δ	delta	d	Π	π	pi	p
Ε	ε	epsilon	e	Ρ	ρ	rho	r, rh
Ζ	ζ	zeta	z	Σ	σ	sigma	s
Η	η	eta	ē	Τ	τ	tau	t
Θ	θ	theta	th	Υ	υ	upsilon	u, y
Ι	ι	iota	i	Φ	φ	phi	ph
Κ	κ	kappa	k	Χ	χ	chi	ch
Λ	λ	lambda	l	Ψ	ψ	psi	ps
Μ	μ	mu	m	Ω	ω	omega	ō

Project Description

Create bilingual exhibition cards for your museum artifacts by writing the name of the artifact both in English and Greek. The process of changing words written in one writing system into another writing system is called transliteration. There are many rules for doing this developed by different linguists, but you can keep the process simple for this activity. Use the chart above to help you. If you need to make up a letter or symbol, be sure to include a key on the exhibit card so everyone understands what you mean.

Ancient Greece © 2006 The Learning Works

Greek Columns

Greek temples were homes for the individual god or goddess who protected the community and were designed to be beautiful tributes to the gods or goddesses. Columns, the pillars that support the roofs of temples, consist of three main parts: the base, the shaft, and the capital. Ancient Greek columns followed one of three architectural forms, called orders.

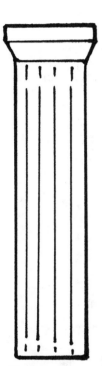

Doric Order

Doric columns are the simplest. The order was developed by the Dorian tribes on the Greek mainland. Doric columns are thick and sturdy and have flutes (grooves) running down the side of the column. The top, or capital, of the column is a simple square. They have no base. An example of a temple that uses Doric columns is the Parthenon in Athens.

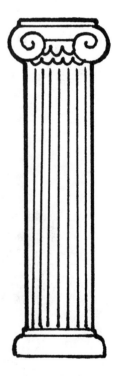

Ionic Order

Ionic columns are taller and more slender than Doric columns. The order was created by the Ionians. The capital is decorated with a scroll-like design called a volute. Ionic columns have a rounded base and usually 24 flutes, more than a Doric column. An example of a temple using the Ionic order is the Erechtheum, built on the Acropolis of Athens.

Corinthian Order

Corinthian columns are very elaborate. They have the fanciest capitals, which are carved with twisting acanthus leaves. The Corinthian order was built to be sturdier than the Ionic order. It was first used in the city-state of Corinth. This was the style that most influenced Roman architecture.

 Ancient Greece © 2006 The Learning Works

Greek Columns *(continued)*

Project Description

The Parthenon in Athens is a good example of a temple that is both famous and beautiful. It was built between 447 and 438 B.C. and was the first building to be constructed on the Acropolis. It had seventeen Doric columns along its length and eight columns along its width. This is an amazing architectural accomplishment. You decide that your museum must have a replica of a beautiful Greek column. Choose an order (Doric, Ionic, Corinthian), sketch the elements that you want to replicate, and then make a model out of plaster. Do your own research to find a temple that used the type of column you made, and include information about the temple on your description card.

Materials

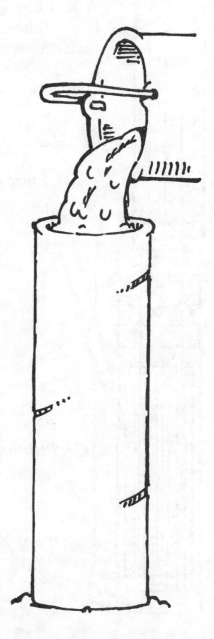

> drawing paper
> plaster of paris
> disposable mixing container like a paper paint bucket
> mixing sticks
> water
> tall, narrow mold for the shaft (paper towel tube, wrapping paper tube, or rolled heavy paper)
> mold for the base (oatmeal container or mold slightly larger in diameter than the shaft)
> mold for the capital (box slightly larger than the shaft, such as a small milk carton or small gift box)
> carving tools such as chisels, dull kitchen knives, nails wrapped in masking tape, old dental tools, pointed nut crackers, nail file
> paper towels
> glue

Directions

1. Choose the type of column you want to make. Make a pattern for the design that you will carve into the hardened plaster.

2. Mix plaster of paris according to the package directions.

3. When the plaster of paris is the right consistency—like sour cream—pour it into the molds. Tap the bottom of each mold on a flat surface to release any trapped air.

Ancient Greece © 2006 The Learning Works

Name: _____

Greek Columns *(continued)*

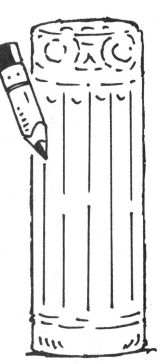

4. The plaster will harden in just a few minutes. When the plaster is ready, peel the mold away and discard the pieces.

5. You'll notice that the plaster may be warm. The warmth indicates that the plaster is soft, so working with the parts of the column is easy at this stage.

6. Use a pencil to sketch a basic outline of your design on the column pieces. Begin carving. Blowing the plaster dust will make your work area messy. Clean up your work area frequently with damp paper towels.

7. Be careful in cleaning up because plaster can clog sink drains. Clean your hands by wiping the plaster on a rag or paper towels, and then rinse in a bucket of water.

Hints

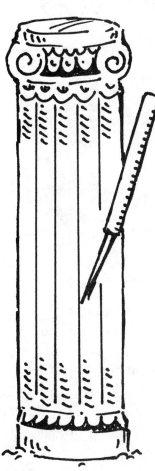

a. Use sculpting tools to make the flutes in the shafts of the columns.

b. For a Doric capital, mold a small amount of plaster in a box which is larger than the top of the shaft, for example a small milk carton or a small gift box. When the plaster is set, peel off the mold and sculpt it into shape. Attach the capital to the shaft with glue.

c. For an Ionic capital, use the same molding technique described for the Doric capital. Then sculpt the scroll shape. Another option is to use white paper rolled into a scroll shape which you can attach to the top of the shaft with glue.

d. For a Corinthian column, make the capital by using a tubular mold. Pour about 2 inches of plaster into the mold. Peel off the mold when the plaster has hardened. Make leaves out of white paper and attach them to the dry plaster with glue. If you have lots of patience, you can carve the leaves into the capital.

e. For the bases of the Ionic and Corinthian columns, pour 1–2 inches of plaster of paris into a tubular mold. The diameter of the mold should be slightly larger than the diameter of the shaft. Peel off the mold when the plaster has hardened. Attach the base to the shaft with glue.

Ancient Greece © 2006 The Learning Works

Name: _____

Greek Coins

The ancient Greeks were some of the earliest people to use money. Each Greek city-state made its own silver coins. The city name was stamped on each coin, along with a picture of something connected with the city like an image of a god or goddess, a hero, or an animal symbol. In Athens, coins were nicknamed "owls" because they showed the head of an owl on one side. Athens was named for the goddess Athena and the owl is the symbol of Athena. At each mint, the weight of the coin was precisely calibrated, though the standard weight of each coin differed from one city-state to the next.

The main coin was the *drachma*. Other coins were the *stater*, the *obol*, and the *tetradrachm*. The *stater* equaled two *drachma*s, the *tetradrachm* was four times the value of a *drachma*, and six *obol*s equaled one *drachma*.

Project Description

The Athens Numismatic Museum was exciting and informative. You never realized how interesting ancient money would be until you learned about its historical, archaeological, and artistic aspects. During your tour you saw thousands and thousands of coins from ancient Greece, many of them depicting insects. One entomologist said that the ancient Greeks minted over 300 different coins with insects. You begin planning a coin display for your museum. You want to include a variety of coins with interesting artistic pictures. Create your coins out of clay and include a short, descriptive overview of their history and the meaning of the art on them. (You can copy ancient Greek coins, or you can design your own coins using ancient Greek designs.)

Ancient Greece © 2006 The Learning Works

Greek Coins *(continued)*

Materials

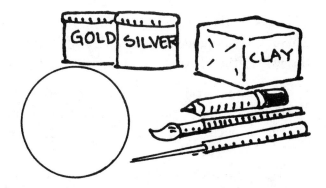

- air-drying clay
- carving tools
- paper circle, 2–3 inches in diameter
- paper and pencil
- silver or bronze paint
- paint brushes

Directions

1. Make a detailed pattern of what you will be drawing on the coin or coins. You may not want to carve the reverse side of the coin but include a drawing of it.

2. If your drawing is complicated, show just the major features on the clay coin.

3. Pat out a small ball of clay to about 1/2 inch thick and slightly larger than the paper circle.

4. Place the circle pattern over the clay and cut around it with a carving tool.

5. Carve the pattern into the clay.

6. When the clay has dried, paint the coin silver or bronze.

Ancient Greece © 2006 The Learning Works

Greek Gods and Goddesses

In Greek mythology, twelve gods and goddesses ruled the universe from atop Mount Olympus. These gods and goddesses, known as "Olympians," came to power after their leader, Zeus, overthrew his father, Kronos.

In ancient Greek art, the Olympian gods and goddesses were often portrayed with a specific set of symbols and attributes. Knowing the symbols of a particular deity becomes especially useful, as it allows one to identify a god or goddess in art.

ZEUS   POSEIDON   HERMES   APOLLO

APHRODITE   ARTEMIS   AESCULARIUS   HERA

Project Description

The curator of the Ancient Greek Museum has invested a great deal of time, money, and effort into setting up new museum exhibits. However, one important exhibit is missing—a display of the important gods and goddesses with their identifying symbols. The curator wants to create such a display and has asked you to help. Choose one of the gods or goddesses to work on for your part of the display. Make sure it is holding or wearing its symbol(s).

Ancient Greece © 2006 The Learning Works

Greek Gods and Goddesses *(continued)*

Materials

aluminum foil
permanent ink marking pens
masking tape
paint and brushes
cardboard
scissors
glue
cloth—old sheets, toweling, ribbons
cardboard

Directions

1. On a sheet of paper, make a plan that details the components of the project.

2. Gently crumple the foil to create the god or goddess figure for your project. If you squeeze too hard, the foil compresses and the figure will get too thin.

3. Use extra pieces of foil to strengthen the arms and legs.

4. Use the masking tape to completely wrap the figure.

5. A thin layer of papier mache can be applied over the masking tape. Otherwise, paint over the masking tape and draw in authentic details. (See pages 12–13 for papier mache directions.)

6. Use cloth or ribbons for clothing and accessories.

7. Make the symbol(s) out of cardboard. Paint and attach the symbol(s) to the figure.

Ancient Greece © 2006 The Learning Works

A Relief Sculpture and Frieze

If you look at the tops of many Greek temples and buildings, you will see a frieze, an important feature of Greek architecture. A frieze is a decorative, horizontal band made of hundreds of slightly raised sculptures (relief sculpture). A frieze usually depicts a significant event in Greek history.

Probably the most famous frieze is the one that was created largely by the sculptor Phidias for the Parthenon in Athens. The carved figures are about a meter high and go in a continuous line around the central chamber of the Parthenon. Most scholars think it depicts the Panathenaic Procession, an important religious event in ancient Athens dedicated to the goddess Athena. Today, parts of the frieze are distributed among the Parthenon, the Acropolis Museum, the British Museum in London, and the Louvre in Paris.

Project Description

Work with a group of students to create a design for an ancient Greek frieze. Each person in the group can create one portion of the frieze. Discuss whether or not the frieze will depict some historical or cultural event or if each student will choose his or her own design. Also, decide if the frieze will be vividly painted like it was during its creation, or if it will be displayed as it is seen today, as white stone. Display the frieze in your museum.

A Relief Sculpture and Frieze *(continued)*

Materials

one 12 x 12 inch piece of heavy cardboard for each section of the frieze
one 12 x 12 inch piece of drawing paper
pencil
aluminum foil
heavy duty masking tape (or duct tape)
scissors
papier mache materials (see pages 12–13)
acrylic paints, either white, off-white, or a variety of colors
paint brushes

Directions

1. On the drawing paper, sketch the outline of the person or animal that will be on your section of the frieze. Cut it out.

2. Place it on the heavy piece of cardboard and tape it down.

3. Position a piece of crumpled aluminum foil over the drawing trying to match the outline as closely as possible. Attach small bits of foil to the main piece to finish difficult parts of the drawing. Attach the foil to the cardboard with tape.

4. Use a thin layer of papier mache to cover the foil figure. (see pages 12–13)

5. Allow the papier mache to dry thoroughly. Paint the frieze either completely in white or in bright colors.

6. When the paint is dry, place the frieze components in the order in which they will hang.

7. Attach the finished frieze to a wall in your museum.

Another way to create a relief sculpture—one that is slightly raised from the flat surface of the cardboard—is to cut out the person or animal from several layers of thick paper and glue them together; craft foam can also be used.

Optional: Create a frieze that resembles those found on Greek vases. Use red butcher paper, about 1½ feet wide. Cut out black silhouettes of Greek warriors, sportmen, and other people or animals, and glue them on the red paper. Add a border of Greek designs on both the top and bottom of the frieze. Hang the frieze at the top of a wall in the museum.

A *Hoplite* Shield

Foot soldiers called *hoplites* were the best-trained soldiers in the ancient Greek army. *Hoplites* were generally citizen-soldiers who served when necessary in defense of their city. Each *hoplite* used a large round shield (*hoplon*), a spear, and a sword, and usually wore a helmet, body armor, and greaves (leg guards).

Hoplites are famous for the use of a phalanx, a military formation where soldiers fought in lines, shoulder to shoulder. In this way each man was protected by the shield of the *hoplite* standing next to him. When they all marched forward together, no enemy spears or arrows could get through their wall of shields. This required good discipline, rigorous training, and precise coordination.

A *hoplon* was about three feet across. The shield was made of several layers: metal, wood, and linen, cloth, or leather. It could weigh as much as twenty pounds. Each *hoplite* chose his own shield design. Shields were decorated with painted designs showing people, animals, or monsters. The designs made it easy to tell one soldier from another. Soldiers often put scary faces on their shields to scare away the enemy.

Project Description

Several renowned ancient Greece scholars will be attending the grand opening of the Ancient Greece Museum. You and your staff want to impress them with your knowledge of Greek warfare, but you also want a colorful display that will attract visitors and be educational at the same time. Study pictures of *hoplons* and then re-create one of them for the museum. You might also want to impress the experts by drawing a *hoplite* in full military regalia to be put on display alongside the shields.

 Ancient Greece © 2006 The Learning Works

A *Hoplite* Shield (continued)

Materials

drawing paper
heavy cardboard, at least 24 x 24 inches
pencil
ruler
scissors
elastic, at least 1 inch wide
masking tape
scratch paper
acrylic paints or marking pens
paint brushes

Directions

1. Use a piece of drawing paper to make the design that you want on your *hoplon*. You can copy one of the ancient *hoplon*s or create one of your own design. Remember to use traditional Greek patterns.

2. Draw a circle that is 24 inches in diameter on the cardboard.

3. Cut out the circle.

4. Draw the design on the shield in pencil and use marking pens or acrylic paints to color in the design.

5. Cut the elastic into two pieces, one five inches and one seven inches long.

6. Tape the elastic to the back of the shield as shown in the drawing. This will be where you put your arm to hold up the shield.

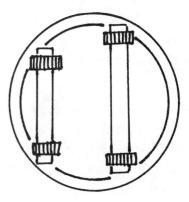

     Ancient Greece © 2006 The Learning Works

Archimedes' Screw

Greece has very few sources of natural water. Water was so scarce in ancient Athens that the Acropolis had a secret staircase that descended into a deep reservoir that held water piped from other springs. This reservoir was constructed to ensure sufficient water supplies in case the city was attacked. Wells, artesian wells, and cisterns were used as water-holders.

Engineering advances like water canals and pipelines made it possible to bring water to a city, rather than always locating a city at the water source. One extraordinary advance was a mechanism for irrigation invented by Archimedes (287–212 B.C.), a Greek mathematician, physicist, and engineer. Called the Archimedes' screw, its basic form consisted of threads fixed to a wooden core enclosed by a cylinder, or tube. It functioned by moving water up the screw and out the top. The threads on the inside collected water and as the tube rotated, the water was brought up and put into a storage tank or water canal. The person running the screw, usually a slave, held onto a rail at the top and used his own muscle power to propel the water upward. The Archimedes' screw is still in use today.

Project Description

Your visit to the Ancient Greek Technology Exhibition at the Technology Museum of Thessaloniki was a highlight of your tour to Greece. There were many displays of ancient Greek inventions, achievements, and technical accomplishments. It was especially interesting learning more about Archimedes who is considered by many to be the best mathematician ever. It inspires you to ask your museum staff to create a model of an Archimedes' screw for display in your Ancient Greek Museum.

Archimedes' Screw *(continued)*

Materials

two-liter plastic water or soda bottle of a
  uniform diameter, i.e., straight-sided
lightweight cardboard like poster board
pencil
paper towel tube
scissors
tape
rice
two bowls of different sizes, one larger
  and deeper than the other

Directions

1. Take a two-liter soda bottle and cut off the top and bottom. An adult should make the initial "poke" in the plastic bottle's top and bottom. You can put the scissors in the hole to cut off the top and bottom.

2. Place this plastic cylinder on a piece of lightweight cardboard and trace around the inside circumference of the cylinder six different times. Cut out the six circles.

3. A paper towel tube will be the center of your screw. Center the tube on your cardboard circles and trace around it.

4. Next cut straight in from the side and cut around the small inside circle. Remove the center creating doughnut-shaped rings.

5. Tape the rings together, end to end, to form a long spiral.

6. Finally, secure the spiral to the paper towel tube by taping it at the top and bottom and several places between. Place the spiral inside the clear plastic cylinder from the soda bottle.

7. Fill the large bowl with rice and place the two bowls next to each other.

8. Place the bottom of your Archimedes' screw in the bowl of rice. Turn the paper towel tube and watch the rice move up the screw and empty into the smaller bowl.

 Ancient Greece © 2006 The Learning Works

Ancient Catapult

Warfare was a normal part of Greek life, and the city-states frequently fought one another. When laying siege to cities, the armies used catapults, flame throwers, battering rams, and other weapons.

The catapult, sometimes called the *ballista*, is a device that hurls heavy spears or shoots arrows with great force over a long distance. It was so important in fighting that catapult shooting became one of the traditional Greek sports used to train the military. It was invented in ancient Greece in 399 B.C. Dionysius the Elder of Syracuse was looking for new weapons. According to ancient historians, Dionysius gathered together skilled craftsmen and engineers and challenged them to invent new war weapons. The best designers were rewarded with high wages and prizes. One of the new inventions was the catapult, and it continued to be a major weapon of warfare for over a thousand years. Later, the Romans added wheels to the catapult for maneuverability, but very little in the design of the machine changed. A double-armed catapult, also called the *trebuchet*, was invented during the Middle Ages.

Project Description

You were the museum's representative at a seminar on the weapons of ancient Greece. During the first workshop, you learned about the advantages that a catapult gave an ancient Greek army. The museum committee on acquisitions wants to include a simple hands-on experimental catapult, one that both children and adults will enjoy using. It should be educational and fun. Include drawings or pictures of an actual catapult in your exhibit.

Ancient Catapult *(continued)*

Materials

block of wood about 4 x 6 inches
    or larger, at least 1½ inches thick
masking tape
pencil
rubber bands
plastic spoons
nail and hammer
cotton balls or crunched foil balls
paint and brushes (optional)

Directions

1. Paint the block of wood. (optional)

2. Use the masking tape to attach the spoon to one end of the block. The bowl of the spoon should face inward toward the wood.

3. Put a rubber band over the spoon and tape it in place just below the bowl of the spoon.

4. Measure the rubber band to where it comes on the top of the block without being stretched. Mark that spot with a pencil. Hammer in a nail at that spot.

5. Take the other end of the rubber band and put it around the nail.

6. Practice shooting cotton balls or crunched foil balls.

Ancient Greece © 2006 The Learning Works

Greek Clothing

(The terminology used for ancient Greek clothing is based on various disciplines, especially art, history, and archaeology. As a result, variations exist.)

Historians and archaeologists have inferred a lot about Greek clothing by studying statues and pictures on pottery. Greek historians like Herodutus gave very detailed descriptions of fashion. If you take a good look at a Greek vase, you will see that most of the people are wearing a *chiton* or tunic. A *chiton* was made from two rectangular pieces of cloth—usually finely spun wool but sometimes linen—sewn or pinned together. It was pulled over the head and tied around the waist. Women and girls wore their *chiton*s long, to the ground, while men and boys gathered them under their belts so that they only hung to their knees. An earlier version of the *chiton*, sometimes called a *peplos*, was folded over at the neck into a deep cuff and secured with big pins on the shoulders. Another piece of clothing, made from a rectangular piece of cloth, was called a *himation*. At first it was used as a cloak, but, later, it was draped more elaborately over the *chiton*.

Most people think that Greek clothing was always white; in actuality, a wide range of colors was common, although commoners were forbidden to wear red *chiton*s in public places. There were also extravagant articles of clothing that were woven with threads of silver and gold.

Most Greeks walked barefoot, especially in the house. When they went out they sometimes wore light leather sandals, or leather boots.

Ancient Greece © 2006 The Learning Works

Greek Clothing *(continued)*

Ancient Greece © 2006 The Learning Works

Name: _____

Greek Clothing *(continued)*

Project Description

Imagine that you are on a tour of ancient Athens. Your tour guide meets you in the *agora*, or marketplace, where you maneuver between stalls of fish, meat, vegetables, pottery, and animals. There are tradesmen everywhere. As you meander through the *agora*, you are observing the clothing that the people are wearing, comparing the different styles and noting how men and women's clothing differs. You want to have a section of your Ancient Greek Museum devoted to clothing. Start by making a simple *chiton*.

Materials

white sheet or similar fabric, about 6 x 4 feet
scissors
yardstick or tape measure
brooches or safety pins
needle and thread (optional)
cording, about 3 feet
fabric paints (optional)

Directions

1. Fold the piece of fabric so that it measures approximately 3 x 4 feet.

2. Lay it flat on a table and use brooches or safety pins to connect the two halves of the fabric together at each shoulder as shown. Leave an opening in the middle for your head.

3. Sew or pin the open side together. (optional)

4. Use the cording to tie around your waist as a belt. Pull up the fabric above your waist, so the *chiton* ends at your knees if you are a boy. Let it hang if you are a girl.

5. Optional: Use fabric paint to decorate the edges and hem of the *chiton* with traditional Greek patterns.

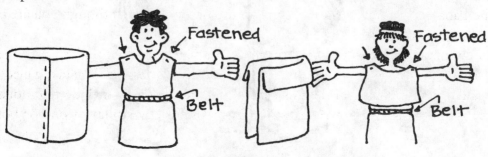

Ancient Greece © 2006 The Learning Works

Brooches

Wealthy Greek women liked to wear lots of jewelry. Brooches and pins were important because they were used to fasten *chitons* together at the shoulders. The women also wore gold and silver necklaces, earrings, and bracelets. Wealthy women also used make-up and had slaves fix their hair in the latest styles.

Chiton styles changed over the years. The Doric *chiton* was long and full and was fastened with many small brooches at the shoulder. The Ionic *chiton* was held together with elaborate pins called *fibulae*. The fabric was draped to create the appearance of sleeves. The enormous width required that eight to ten *fibulae* were needed to fasten the top edge, leaving an openwork seam on either side of the neck.

Project Description

You continue your imaginary tour of Athens. Your guide meets you early in the morning and you walk up the Panathenaic Way, from the *agora* to the Acropolis. Even though you are excited to finally see the Parthenon, the goal of this tour is to observe the types of brooches people use to fasten their clothing. You need to include a brooch or pin in the clothing display in the Ancient Greece Museum, so you need to gather as many design ideas as possible. You take a piece of drawing paper and sketch a couple of designs that you particularly like. Include traditional ancient Greek designs and patterns. Now you can begin making a clay replica of one or both of the brooches.

Brooches *(continued)*

Materials

- sketching paper
- pencil
- air-drying clay
- glue gun (adult supervision required)
- large craft safety pins
- carving tools

Directions

1. Make a sketch of the traditional design that you want to use for your brooch.

2. Mold a piece of clay into a circle about 1 to 2 inches in diameter and about 1/2 inch thick.

3. Carve your design in the clay.

4. Let the brooch dry completely.

5. Glue a safety pin to the back with a hot glue gun. Remember to have adult supervision for this part of the activity. When the glue is completely cool, the brooch is ready to use or display in your museum.

6. If you plan to use these clay brooches to fasten a *chiton* or *peplos*, you will need to make between 8 and 10 of them. You can also use a combination of brooches and safety pins for the fastenings.

 Ancient Greece © 2006 The Learning Works

Name: _____

Greek Vases

The best Greek pottery was made in Athens, where a high-quality clay was found. This clay fired well to a beautiful reddish-brown color. The Greeks had approximately twenty different vase styles, each with its own function. Each storage, funerary, cosmetic, or wine vase was a unique work of art.

There are various styles of decoration in vase painting, but the two main styles are the black-figure technique and red-figure technique. The black-figure style is called that because the people and animals are black, and the background is red. In the red-figure style, on the other hand, the people and animals are red, and the background is black. Soon after 500 B.C., the red-figure technique took over. The figures of gods and animals were now left in the reddish-brown clay and the background was painted in with a clay solution that turned black in the firing process.

With both techniques, the potter first shaped the vessel on a wheel. Most sizeable pots were made in sections. Sometimes the neck and body were thrown separately. The foot was often attached later.

Project Description

An ancient Greek museum is not complete without a section dedicated to beautiful pottery vases. Choose one of the following options to create a vase fit for any museum—or try both options.

A. An etching is usually done on glass or metal plates by using a sharp tool to make the image. You have been given the challenge of creating a beautiful ancient Greek vessel etching by using the same method, only substituting paper for the glass or metal.

B. An easier, but equally beautiful, project is to create the vase from construction paper and black ink.

Ancient Greece © 2006 The Learning Works

Greek Vases *(continued)*

Materials for Option A

orange, rust, or red-orange wax
    crayons

India ink or diluted black tempera

drop of dishwashing liquid

paint brush

white drawing paper 8½ x 11 or
    9 x 12 inches

stencils pre-cut by teacher in the
    shapes of different vases (optional)

ruler

pencil

scissors

sharp objects such as a nail, cuticle
    stick, toothpicks, and clay
    sculpting tools for scratching
    through the ink or tempera

newspapers

construction paper, larger than the
    drawing paper

Directions

1. Research ancient Greek vases, and choose a shape that you think will make an appealing vase. Make a sketch of the outline of the vase (or use the stencil). Use a ruler to create repeated geometric patterns. In the middle, or in the largest part of the vase, draw a simple scene from Greek life—a musician, sports figure, animal, or a god or goddess, etc.

2. Place newspaper on your workspace.

3. Cover the entire surface of the drawing paper with a thick layer of orange, rust, or red-orange crayons.

4. On the uncolored side of the sheet of paper, draw your vase or trace around the stencil. Cut around the outline.

5. With the orange side up, brush India ink or diluted black tempera over the entire waxed surface. A drop of dishwashing liquid helps the ink stick to the crayons. The crayons may show through a little under the ink.

6. Referring to your design from Step 1, use a sharp object to scratch through the black layer to reveal the orange layer underneath. Continue until you have achieved the design that you want.

7. Use a thin pointed permanent ink marking pen to outline facial features or other designs on the vase. (optional)

8. Mount the etched vase on contrasting colored construction paper and display in your museum.

Greek Vases *(continued)*

Materials for Option B

 drawing paper
 pencil
 black construction paper, 9 x 12 inches
 orange construction paper, 9 x 12 inches
 black ink or a thin pointed permanent marking pen
 scissors
 glue
 templates for vase shape (optional)

Directions

1. Research ancient Greek vases, and choose a shape that you think will make an appealing vase. Make a sketch of the outline of the vase (or use the stencil). Use a ruler to create repeated geometric patterns. In the middle, or in the largest part of the vase, draw a simple scene from Greek life—a musician, sports figure, animal, or a god or goddess, etc.

2. Draw the outline of the vase on the orange paper (or use the stencil). Make it as large as possible.

3. Referring to your design from Step 1, use a black pen or a permanent ink marking pen to create your ancient Greek pattern on the orange paper.

4. Cut out the vase and clue it onto the black construction paper.

      Ancient Greece © 2006 The Learning Works

Name: _____

Amphoras

Amphoras, *pelike*s, and *hydria*s are ancient Greek storage containers used for oil, wine, honey, corn, water, etc. One of the most popular containers was the amphora which had a flared neck and two handles, usually located towards the top of the pot. Potters produced amphoras in large numbers. More than 1,000 could be placed on a merchant ship to be traded or sold at faraway ports. Smaller amphoras were probably used to store perfume.

Some amphoras were decorated in beautiful designs. Others were plain, perhaps with the names of rulers or potters stamped on the handles.

Project Description

The Panathenaic festival, a religious festival honoring Athena, the patron goddess of Athens, was held every four years. It included athletic and musical competitions. Amphoras were prizes at the Panathenaic Games. They were filled with olive oil from the sacred trees of Athena. The winner of a chariot race once won 140 amphoras. The pottery prizes were decorated with pictures or symbols representing the contest, the goddess Athena, and sometimes the chief official presiding at the event. Pretend that you have been commissioned to create a prize amphora for the upcoming Panathenaic Games. You decide to create one with pictures of athletes, Athena, and other symbols and objects that will honor the winner.

Ancient Greece © 2006 The Learning Works

Amphoras *(continued)*

Materials

- air-drying clay
- marking pens or acrylic paints—red, black, white
- drawing paper
- paint brushes
- sculpting tools (see p. 14)

Directions

1. Make a detailed sketch of the amphora that you want to make. Your design should be worthy of being presented at the Panathenaic Games.

2. Work the clay until it is soft and pliable, and form it into a ball.

3. Begin to mold the clay into the amphora by putting your finger inside almost to the bottom. Squeeze the neck to make it narrower, and flair out the lip portion to make the top of the amphora.

4. Create the bottom with a narrower, pointed bottom. You might want to make a flat-bottomed amphora because it will be easier to stand up in your museum.

5. Add handles by making clay snakes and adhering them to the top of the amphora.

6. Use your finger or a craft stick to make the bottom rim of the amphora.

7. When the clay has dried and hardened, apply your design with marking pens or acrylic paints.

8. Write a story describing the design of the amphora and watching it being presented to a famous athlete. Display the story with the amphora in the museum. (optional)

Ancient Greece © 2006 The Learning Works

Olympian Plate

The people of ancient Greece valued excellence and admired aesthetic, intellectual, and athletic achievement. They believed in the value of sports as training for warfare and as a way of honoring the gods. Rivalries grew up among the city-states, and representatives competed vigorously on both the athletic field and the battlefield.

The ancient Greeks chose Olympia as one site for their athletic contests. Later the events held there became known as the Olympic Games. The first recorded Olympic event was held in 776 B.C. In the beginning, the games lasted only one day, but gradually more events were added, resulting in the games lasting for five days. The main events were running, the pentathlon, jumping, discus, javelin, wrestling, boxing, chariot racing, and horse racing.

All Greeks who were free citizens and who had not committed a major crime had the right to take part in the Olympic Games. Women were not entitled to take part, except as owners in the horse races, and were strictly prohibited from watching the games.

The victors enjoyed great honors and when they returned to their cities, their fans pulled down part of the walls for them to enter. They were also given special privileges and high offices.

The Olympic Games were held in Greece every four years for nearly twelve centuries. Not even wars were allowed to interfere with this schedule; during the month of the Olympic Festival, a truce was declared between all warring city-states. The games were banned in A.D. 394 with the rise of the Roman Empire.

Project Description

Create an Olympian plate that is worthy of the winner of an event as grueling as the pentathlon, a five-event contest in which athletes had to perform well in the long jump, the discus throw, the javelin throw, wrestling, and boxing.

Name: _____

Olympian Plate *(continued)*

Materials

paper and pencil
air-drying clay (use red-orange clay, if available)
sculpting tools (see page 14)
an old dinner plate
small amount of oil or Vaseline
plastic wrap, enough to cover the back of the plate
plastic knife
acrylic paint, tempera, or permanent marking pens
paint brushes

Directions

1. Decide on the athletic event for the plate. Make a sketch of the design and include a drawing of the athlete and a picture or symbol of a god or goddess. Put a traditional Greek pattern around the rim of the plate.

2. Turn the dinner plate over, rub the back with Vaseline or oil, and place a piece of plastic wrap over the oiled plate.

3. Roll or pat the clay into a piece large enough to cover the back of the plate. It should be a uniform thickness, about 1/4 inch. Place this onto the back of the plate and press firmly. Use the plastic knife to trim around the plate and remove any excess clay.

4. When the clay dries completely, remove it from the dinner plate.

5. Pencil in your design.

6. Use acrylic paints, tempera, or permanent marking pens to color the design.

Ancient Greece © 2006 The Learning Works

Olympic Wreath

Competitors and spectators from all over Greece went to Olympia for the Olympics. Olympia wasn't a town, so people had to camp there. There were religious festivals and feasts. Participants took an oath that they had trained for the games and that they would not cheat.

A winning athlete's only official reward was a wreath of olive leaves cut from a sacred olive tree. Olive trees, which supplied the Greeks with olive oil, olives, a cleaning agent for bathing, and a base for perfumes, were an important resource in the rocky and dry country. Although a winner did not receive money at the Olympics, he was treated much like a modern sports celebrity by his home city. Statues were raised in his honor, and he was given special privileges.

In the ancient games, olive branches for the winners' wreaths were taken from a sacred grove in Olympia. In the 2004 Summer Olympics in Athens, the victors were also crowned with olive wreaths, taken from olive groves around Greece. The organizers felt that reviving the ancient symbol of the olive wreath was a reminder of what the spirit of sport should be.

Project Description

Make a wreath to place along side a drawing of an Olympic champion or to wear at your museum events.

Ancient Greece © 2006 The Learning Works

Olympic Wreath *(continued)*

Materials

piece of ribbon, about 1 x 22 inches
heavy cardboard strip, about 1 x 22 inches
scissors
glue
stapler
hot glue gun (optional)
ruler
leaf template (optional)
construction paper in various shades of green
real or artificial leaves (optional)

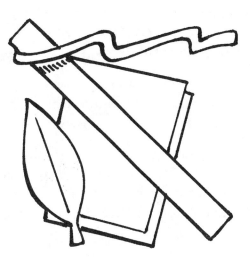

Directions

1. Make outlines of at least twenty leaves using the leaf template, or make sketches if you prefer, on the construction paper. Make sure you have a stem on each leaf and cut them out. Or, gather real or artifical leaves and cut them, if necessary, so they can be attached to the headband.

2. Carefully glue the ribbon to the cardboard strip creating your headband. Let dry thoroughly.

3. Attach your leaves to the headband. There are different ways to do this. You can cut slits about 1/2 to 1 inch apart, and poke the stems of the leaves through the slit; staple, glue, or tape them so they won't come out. Or, you can staple or glue them directly to the headband. You might find that a hot glue gun works best for this method. Remember to have an adult help with the hot glue gun.

4. Fit the headband around your head and staple. Cut off any extra length.

Ancient Greece © 2006 The Learning Works

Greek Fresco

Fresco is the art of painting on plastered walls. This medium was one of the ancient Greek civilization's major art forms. Interiors of villas and palaces were covered with fanciful impressions of life and nature in the Greek world.

To make a fresco, artists prepared a wall with a thin layer of white lime plaster. Then the artist outlined the main features and sketched in important details. Next, the colors were applied, often while the surface was still moist so that they soaked in and made the painted images more durable.

Fresco painting dates back to 1500 B.C. Two more recent fresco painters are Michelangelo and Diego Rivera. Michelangelo painted beautiful frescoes on the walls and ceiling of the Sistine Chapel in Vatican City. Diego Rivera painted frescoes in Mexico. Each artist used similar techniques but developed his own style and themes.

Project Description

You've been conducting research to learn more about ancient Greek frescoes. Polygnotus of Thasos was a Greek painter who was as famous as Michelangelo. The most important of his paintings were frescoes in a building erected at Delphi. Today none of his work survives. Using your expertise in ancient Greek art, design a portion of a fresco; include drawings and symbols which represent the culture of the times.

Ancient Greece © 2006 The Learning Works

Greek Fresco *(continued)*

Materials

sketching paper
pencil
plaster of paris
disposable paint bucket for mixing plaster
wooden paint mixer stick
shoebox lid, or a box of similar size
tempera or acrylic paints
craft sticks for spreading plaster
paint brushes

Directions

1. Make a sketch of your fresco. Keep the design simple. Animals, plants, symbols of gods and goddesses, geometric patterns, and silhouette figures will work well.

2. Mix the plaster of paris in the disposable bucket with the paint stick.

3. Pour the plaster into the box lid.

4. Use a craft stick or other tool to smooth the plaster. Make the surface as smooth as possible.

5. Begin to paint onto the plaster surface when the plaster is almost dry, but still damp. The more layers of paint you put on the fresco, the brighter it will be. As the plaster dries, the pigments from the paint set into it. Apply additional layers of paint if the colors fade as the plaster dries.

6. Gently remove the mold from around the plaster. Let the fresco dry thoroughly.

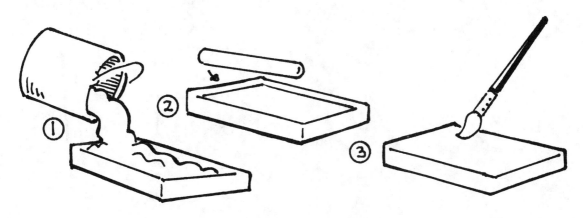

Ancient Greece © 2006 The Learning Works

Name: _____

Greek Masks

There were two main forms of Greek drama, tragedies and comedies. A tragedy concerned heroes, kings, and gods who suffer bad fortune. Comedy concerned average people who enjoy a transition from bad circumstances to good.

Tragedies were part of a religious festival to Dionysus. On each of three days, three tragedies were presented by the same writer. A panel of judges awarded a prize for the best group of plays. Aeschylus and Sophocles usually won when they presented plays. Aeschylus (525–456 B.C.), called the "father of tragedy," wrote about 90 tragedies. He was the first to use a second actor on the stage. Sophocles (496–406 B.C.) wrote about 125 tragedies. He was the first to use a third actor. Euripedes (480–406 B.C.) wrote approximately 90 plays. His tragedies are about men, not gods. Aristophanes was the greatest comic writer of his day. He made fun of political leaders, philosophers, and other literary figures.

Greek plays had certain characteristics. A chorus consisting of three to fifty people—all men— were masked and in costume. Also, all of the actors were men who took several parts, if necessary. The writer composed the music and the dance as well as the text, directed the production, and trained the chorus. The actors didn't have to worry about facial expressions because masks were used. Special emotions were expressed on the mask, so the audience knew if a character was happy, upset, tired, or scared. A mask was used to show the change in character or mood. Most masks were made of stiffened linen, cork, carved wood, or leather. To create the shape of the mask, the artist molded material much like papier mache around a marble face. The mouth hole was made large enough to help amplify voices.

Ancient Greece © 2006 The Learning Works

Greek Masks *(continued)*

Project Description

A scroll is delivered to you. You unroll it and read:

> *Citizens of Athens, you are invited to join in the celebration of the Festival of Dionysus.*
> *We will have dramatic competitions, a grand procession, revelry, religious ceremonies,*
> *and the crowning of victors. However, Citizens, we need your help in making the masks*
> *for the tragedies and comedies. Bring your completed mask to the theater.*

You roll up the scroll and immediately begin sketching a mask that you hope will be accepted and used in a theater production. Whether it is used or not, it will appear in the Ancient Greek Museum.

Materials

    drawing paper
    pencil
    round balloon
    papier mache materials (see pages 12–13 for more
        information)
    acrylic paints, tempera, or permanent marking pens
    paint brushes
    assorted yarns, furs, cloth, and other trims and decorations
    scissors
    sand paper
    elastic, about fourteen inches (optional)

Ideas for masks

    Gods and goddesses
    Political leaders
    Mythological monsters: cyclopes, gorgons, sirens, hydras
    Muses

Ancient Greece © 2006 The Learning Works

Greek Masks *(continued)*

Directions

1. Draw a design for your mask. Emphasize smile or frown wrinkles, cheeks, eyebrows in exaggerated facial expressions, etc.

2. Blow up the balloon and knot the opening.

3. Papier mache over the front and sides of the balloon. Directions for papier mache can be found on pages 12–13.

4. Make a mixture of tiny bits of newspaper and glue. Use this mixture to mold features like eyebrow ridges, cheekbones, and other facial features. Press the features onto the mask.

5. When the papier mache is dry, pop the balloon and remove the mask.

6. Sand the mask lightly with sandpaper so the paints will adhere better.

7. Determine the distance between the eyes. They should be about a third of the way down the mask, and centered from side to side. Experiment on the sketch, if necessary. Cut out the eye and mouth openings.

8. Sketch your design from Step 1 onto the papier mache mask.

9. Paint the mask and glue on decorations.

10. Punch a hole on each side of the mask. Thread the elastic through the holes and then knot each end. (optional)

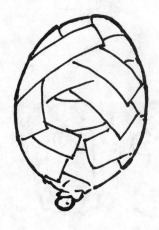  

Ancient Greece © 2006 The Learning Works

Trojan Horse

More than 3,000 years ago in what is now Turkey, there was a walled city called Troy. No one could enter the city except through a heavily guarded gate. The people of Troy waged war on the Greeks, and when they kidnapped Helen, wife of a Spartan prince, the Athenians teamed up with the Spartans and declared war on the Trojans. The Greeks soon discovered that the walls of Troy were impenetrable. They decided to get through the walls by using trickery.

A huge wooden horse was ordered built. Its insides were to be hollow so that soldiers could hide within it. The Greeks presented the horse to the Trojans and pretended to sail away. The Trojans, cautious at first, finally accepted the gift and wheeled it inside the city. That night, the Greeks hiding inside the horse climbed down and ran to the beach. They lit a signal fire and the Greek ships sailed back. The Greeks broke into the city and killed nearly all of the Trojans. They burned Troy and then sailed home with Helen.

For many years, no one really knew if the city of Troy ever existed. Homer, a Greek poet, wrote about it in a famous poem called the *Iliad*. Two thousand years later a German archaeologist named Heinrich Schliemann read the *Iliad* and used the clues in it to discover the site of the ancient city. He found many things to prove that the ancient city really did exist.

Project Description

Whether or not the Trojan War really occurred is probably an unanswerable question. We know that such a war did take place around a city that quite likely was Troy, that Troy was destroyed, but beyond that it's all speculation. The poet, Homer, who lived centuries after the time of the Trojan War, told the story in the *Iliad* and the *Odyssey*. He likely telescoped 200 years of conflict into a single 10-year war. Today, visitors to the area see an imaginative replica of the Trojan Horse built by the Turkish government. It reminds visitors of the rich history of the region. Make your own replica of the horse. Since no one knows what it looked like—or even if it was real—you can be creative in your design.

Trojan Horse (continued)

Materials

  drawing paper
  pencil
  cardboard boxes of various sizes
  paper tubes of various sizes
  poster board
  masking tape
  two dowels
  papier mache materials, see pages 12–13
  brown and black paint and paint brushes
  black marking pen
  four wheels made from clay
  two dowels for the axles; the size will
      depend on how big the horse is
  masking tape

Directions

1. Make a sketch of the Trojan Horse that you want to make.

2. Choose a box or lid for the base of the horse. This will determine the size of the horse.

3. Collect the boxes and tubes you need for the body, the neck, the head, four legs, and the tail. If you don't have a box for part of the construction, cut and fold pieces of the poster board to the size that you need.

4. Tape all of the parts together with masking tape. Work with a partner to make the taping easier.

5. Cover the entire horse and platform with a thin layer of papier mache. (Refer to pages 12–13 for more information on papier mache.)

6. When the papier mache is thoroughly dry, paint the horse with brown paint. Outline features with black marking pen or black paint.

7. Make four wheels out of clay. Measure the dowels so that they are slightly larger than the base of the horse. Cut the dowels to fit. Put a wheel on each end of the dowel. Place the horse on the dowels and use masking tape to anchor them to the base.

Ancient Greece © 2006 The Learning Works

Mosaic Pictures

The creation of a mosaic is a labor-intensive artistic technique that produces a picture using small pieces of tile, pebbles, or stone. These small objects are arranged into a pattern to create a design or picture. The word *mosaic* is derived from Greek and means "patient work, worthy of the Muses."

Well-to-do Greeks had their floors covered in elaborate mosaics depicting animals, monsters, myths, and geometric and floral patterns. The pictures were usually set within a traditional Greek border. Early mosaics were made with natural pebbles, limited mainly to black for the background and white for the figures, set into mortar. A few stones of different colors were included to improve the effect.

Later, Greek artists made more complicated mosaics. Some of them even appeared as though they were painted. The artists used small cubes cut from stone, glass, or baked clay to have a greater range of color.

Project Description

You are amazed by the intricate designs of the mosaics you saw on your tour of Greece. One of the finest pebble mosaics was at the archaeological museum in Pella. The mosaics were of Dionysus riding a panther, a lion-hunt, and a pair of centaurs. At the Archaeological Museum of Corinth, one of the earliest preserved Greek mosaics was on exhibit. It was a representation of griffins devouring a horse. You are anxious to try your hand at making an ancient Greek–style mosaic using chips of paper or seeds instead of tiles, pebbles, and glass.

You may make a mosaic using paper, seeds, and/or beans. Choose one of these subject ideas for your mosaic: a god or goddess, a Greek temple, a Greek column, a *hoplon* (shield), animals, monsters, geometric patterns, floral patterns, a silhouette of a figure, Greek alphabet letters, masks, features from nature like mountains, rivers, clouds, lightning, etc.

Mosaic Pictures *(continued)*

Paper Mosaic
Materials

    drawing paper or graph paper
    pencil
    gray or white poster board or other thick paper
    construction paper, paint chip samples, or other
        beautifully colored papers
    glue
    scissors

Directions

1. Make a sketch of your design in the same size as the actual mosaic that you will make. Keep your design simple. Use graph paper if that is easier. Transfer your design to the poster board.

2. Cut just enough paper tiles to begin the project. Cut more as you need them. Try to keep them the same size, about 1/2 inch to 1 inch square.

3. Put a tiny dot of glue on the backside of the paper tile and place it on the poster board. As you proceed from tile to tile, leave a tiny space between each square. You should be able to see the poster board or paper showing between each paper tile. This represents the mortar or grout of a Greek mosaic. The squares should not overlap or be on top of one another.

Ancient Greece © 2006 The Learning Works

Mosaic Pictures *(continued)*

Seed or Bean Mosaic

Materials

drawing paper

pencil

pumpkin seeds, dried beans, lentils, or similar small seeds or
beans

tempera paint in a variety of colors

several paper bowls or shallow containers

newspaper or waxed paper

gray or white poster board

glue

Directions

1. Make a sketch of your design in the same size as the actual mosaic that you will make.
Figure out the colors that you want to use and where they will be placed. Keep the design
simple. Transfer your design to the poster board.

2. Divide the seeds among paper bowls, one bowl for each color. Add a bit of paint to the
bowl and stir or mix until all seeds are covered. Do this for each color. Spread the seeds on
newspaper or waxed paper to dry. You can also leave dried beans in their natural state and
they will look very much like the pebbles used in some of the early Greek mosaics.

3. When the seeds are dry, use glue to attach them to the mosaic design on the poster board.

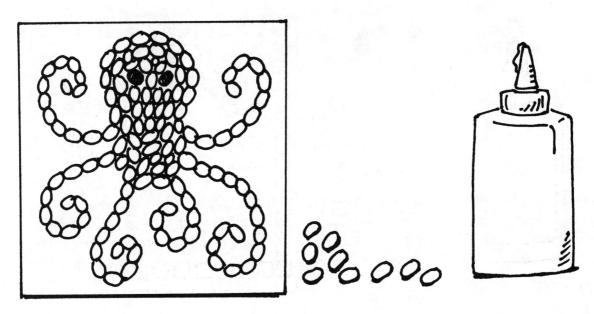

 Ancient Greece © 2006 The Learning Works

Model of Ancient Athens

No city has contributed more to civilization than Athens. It is the place where Socrates, Plato, Aeschylus, Sophocles, Euripides, and many others were born, and it is the place where democracy began.

Tourists to ancient Athens would notice, first of all, the Acropolis with the Parthenon rising high in the center of the city. First, though, they would wander through the *agora*, or market-place, between stalls where fish, meat, vegetables, pottery, and animals were sold and displayed. They would edge their way around groups of men arguing politics and philosophy. The tour would probably continue through the gymnasium where men and boys exercised and trained for athletic competitions, and past the Theater of Dionysus where all the important tragedies and comedies were staged. Then the tourists would follow the Panathenaic Way which led from the town center to the Acropolis, on the hilltop above the town. At the top, everyone would gaze in awe at the sight of the beautiful white marble temples and breathtaking statues.

Project Description

You meet with your staff to discuss ways to represent the beauty and history of ancient Athens. After a lengthy discussion, you decide that your museum needs a model of Athens. The model should include the Acropolis with its important buildings; the *agora*; the Theater of Dionysus; and the Panathenaic Way. Add other important sites that you think are important. Be prepared to take museum visitors on tours of the city.

Ancient Greece © 2006 The Learning Works

Model of Ancient Athens *(continued)*

Materials

sketching paper

pencil

plywood or heavy board,
    about 18 inches square

papier mache materials
    (see pages 12–13 for instructions)

masking tape

clay

foil or newspapers

posterboard, cardboard, or small boxes

tempera or acrylic paints and brushes

glue

scissors

marking pens

plastic toy figures and plants (optional)

ground foam, lichen moss, and other
    scenery items purchased from
    hobby stores (optional)

Directions

1. Decide what you will include in your model of ancient Athens, and whether or not you will make an individual model or a group model. If you are doing a group model, it is important to plan carefully so that the separate pieces fit together properly.

2. Make a map of what you will include in your model. Reproduce it onto the plywood or heavy board so that you will know where to make hills and other land formations.

3. Use crumpled aluminum foil or newspaper to make the land formations. Cover with at least two layers of papier mache. Let dry and paint.

4. Use a pencil to lightly draw where you want to place structures and geographical and landscaping features.

5. Paint the surfaces showing any geographical and landscaping features you want to include.

6. Temples and other buildings can be made out of cardboard or small boxes. You may want to paint or papier mache the structures.

7. Use foil or clay to create figures and other three-dimensional objects that you want to include. See pages 14–15 for instructions.

8. Glue the structures and figures to the base of the model. Add optional scenery items if you want.

Water Clock

The Greeks didn't have the "tick tick" of a mechanical clock to remind them of passing time; instead they heard the "drip drip" of the *clepsydra*, or water clock. A *clepsydra* relied on the steady rising or falling of water level in a container to indicate the passage of time. A simple version of a *clepsydra* consisted of a large vessel that had a small hole located near the base and a graduated stick, like a ruler, attached to a floating base. The hole would be plugged while the urn was being filled with water, and then the stick would be inserted into the urn. The passage of time was measured as the stick descended farther into the urn. This was not an automatic machine. Someone had to pour the water in.

These early water clocks were used when equal measurements of time needed to be established. For example, if two orators were to be allotted the same amount of time to speak before an assembly, a water clock of this nature would have been constructed for the occasion. To ensure that both the plaintiff and defendant would have an equal amount of time to make their cases, the Athenian courts used water clocks. The speaker could tell when his time was running out by a change in water level.

In the second century B.C., Ctesibius, an engineer, improved the *clepsydra* so that it could mark the hours. He put wheels into the water clock so that the clock could run itself. It consisted of four major parts: a vessel for providing a constant supply of water, a reservoir and notched flotation rod, a display, and a device for adjusting the flow of water into the vessel.

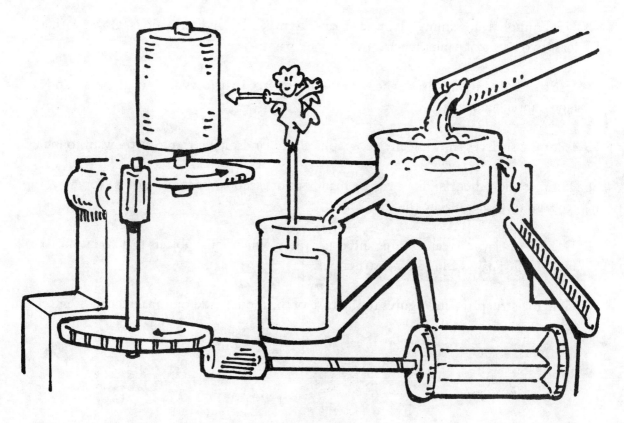

Ancient Greece © 2006 The Learning Works

Water Clock *(continued)*

Project Description

A museum committee on acquisitions made the decision to include a hands-on exhibit where both children and adults can experiment with an ancient Greek artifact. They want the exhibit to be both educational and fun. You decide that a simple water clock would be perfect, and the committee agrees. Make the water clock and display it in your museum. Be prepared for spills so have towels handy!

Materials

rubber bands

marking pens

two identical transparent containers, for example one-liter plastic soft-drink bottles with the tops cut off

piece of poster board about 1 inch wide and the same height as the containers

small nail or thumbtack

hammer

ruler

box or brick the same height as the containers

clock with a second hand

construction paper

pitcher of water

glue

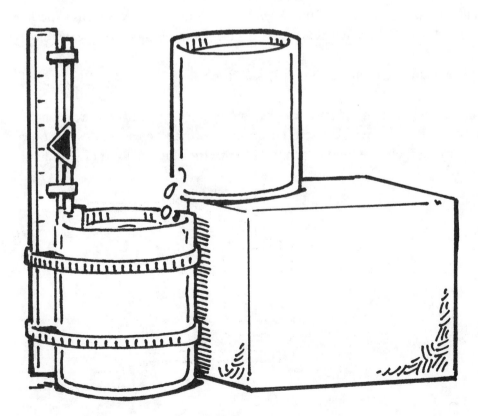

  Ancient Greece © 2006 The Learning Works

Water Clock *(continued)*

Directions

1. Use the nail and hammer to make a tiny hole in the side of one of the containers as close to the bottom as possible. Make the hole small enough so the water only drips out.

2. Use a permanent marking pen to draw a line about 1 inch below the top of the container with the hole. This will be the water level mark so that the clock will always start with the same amount of water.

3. Place the container with the hole in it on top of the brick or box with about 1/3 of the container hanging over the edge.

4. Use the rubber bands to attach the piece of poster board to the other container. This will be your measuring guide.

5. Arrange this container so that water will drip into it from the upper container.

6. Have your ruler and marking pen ready, and fill the top container with water up to the water level mark.

7. Watch the clock and when one minute has passed, mark the water level in the lower container on the poster board and label it "1." Continue on with this process marking every minute until the water is gone. You have just calibrated your water clock.

8. Try it again and see if the timing is the same.

9. Some of the ancient Greek water clocks used pottery jars for the water containers. Decorate your containers to resemble jars by drawing shapes and designs on construction paper, cutting them out, and attaching them to the container either with glue or rubber bands.

Ancient Greece © 2006 The Learning Works

Festival Mural

Ancient Greek artists painted the walls of public buildings, particularly temples. But the paintings were so fragile that hardly any paintings of this kind have survived. Experts get some idea of what the paintings must have looked like by studying the designs on Greek vases.

Some wonderful wall murals were found recently by archaeologists on the Macedonian plain. The actual location is identified as Aigai, the first capital city of Macedon where Philip, the father of Alexander the Great, was murdered in 336 B.C. The archaeological mound contained three large tombs. The murals found in the tombs are exciting examples of Greek painting from the classical period. The subjects included a painting of a two-horse chariot; a painting of the goddess Persephone and the god Hades in his chariot; and a hunting scene.

Project Description

By the seventh century B.C., Greek art showed a focus on motion. Figures, like mythological heroes and athletes, run, crawl, wrestle, or dance. The paintings relate entire stories of Greek heroes and gods, the glories of monarchs, and explanations for how the world was created. You and the museum staff want to create a class mural that will represent the Greek wall murals that were lost over time. Include figures in action, a story or stories about ancient Greek heroes, and other details that you think will make an authentic mural.

Festival Mural *(continued)*

Materials

    research materials, if necessary
    white art paper or brown wrapping paper, 36 inches to 46
       inches wide
    bright acrylic or tempera paints and brushes
    black marking pens
    stapler or tape

Directions

1. Make a class plan for the mural. Discuss how much space each student will need; whether or not the mural will be a coordinated group mural or many independent scenes; and what the mural will portray.

2. Staple or tape the mural paper on a flat surface in the classroom.

3. Work independently or with a partner to make a preliminary sketch of your portion of the mural. Try to include at least one Greek god or goddess in your plans.

4. Using a pencil, lightly draw in the figures, plants, animals, symbols, and geometric patterns on the mural paper.

5. Paint the figures and use marking pens to add details.

Ancient Greece © 2006 The Learning Works